The Pursuit of the Ivory Poachers: KENYA

BOOK 6

Join Secret Agent Jack Stalwart on his other adventures:

The Escape of the Deadly Dinosaur: USA

Book ①

The Search for the Sunken Treasure: AUSTRALIA

Book ②

The Mystery of the Mona Lisa: FRANCE

Book ③

The Caper of the Crown Jewels: ENGLAND

Book ④

The Secret of the Sacred Temple: CAMBODIA

Book ⑤

The Pursuit of the Ivory Poachers: KENYA

Elizabeth Singer Hunt

Illustrated by Brian Williamson

Weinstein Books

Printed in the United States of America. For information address
Weinstein Books, 22 Cortlandt Street, New York, NY 10007.

ISBN: 978-1-60286-021-6

First Edition

10 9 8

For my parents, who, like me,
love the African plains

THE WORLD

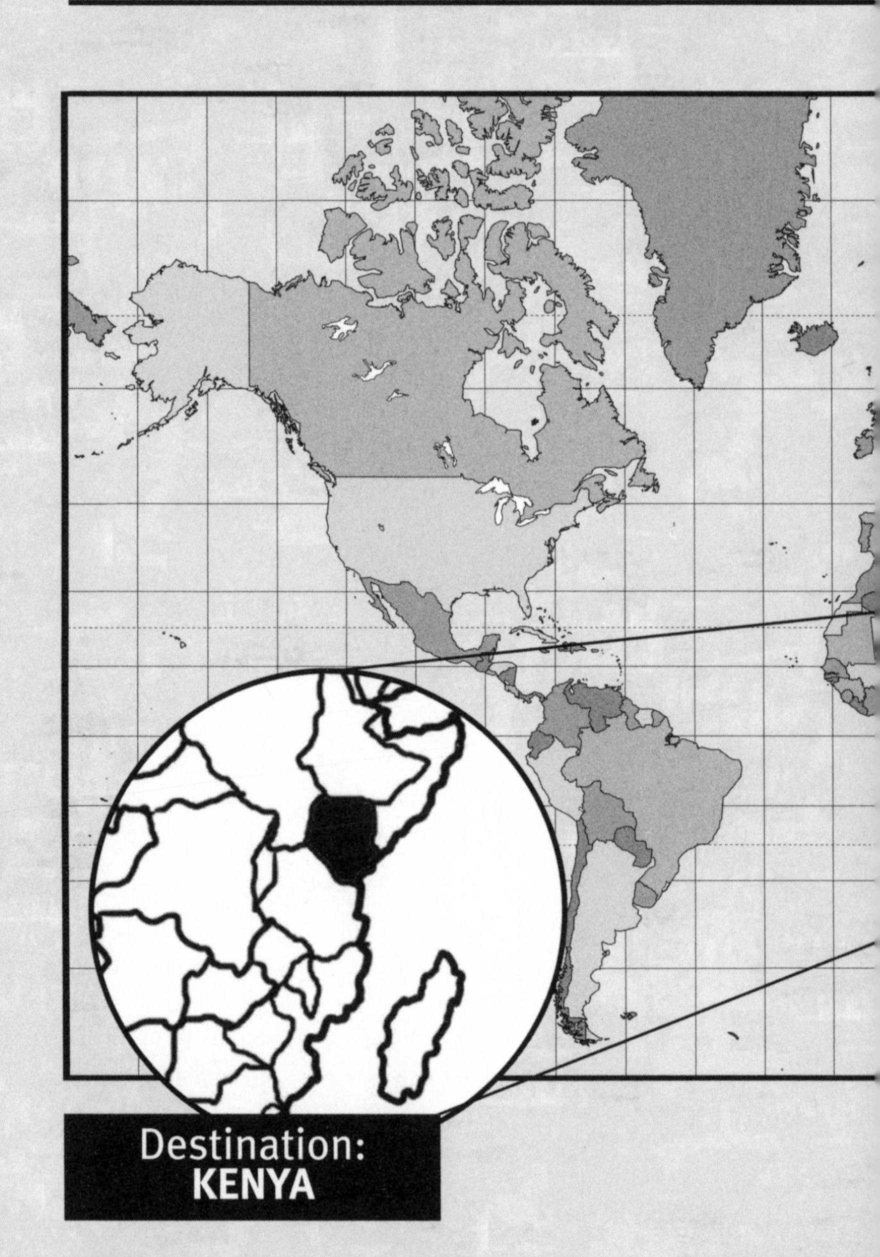

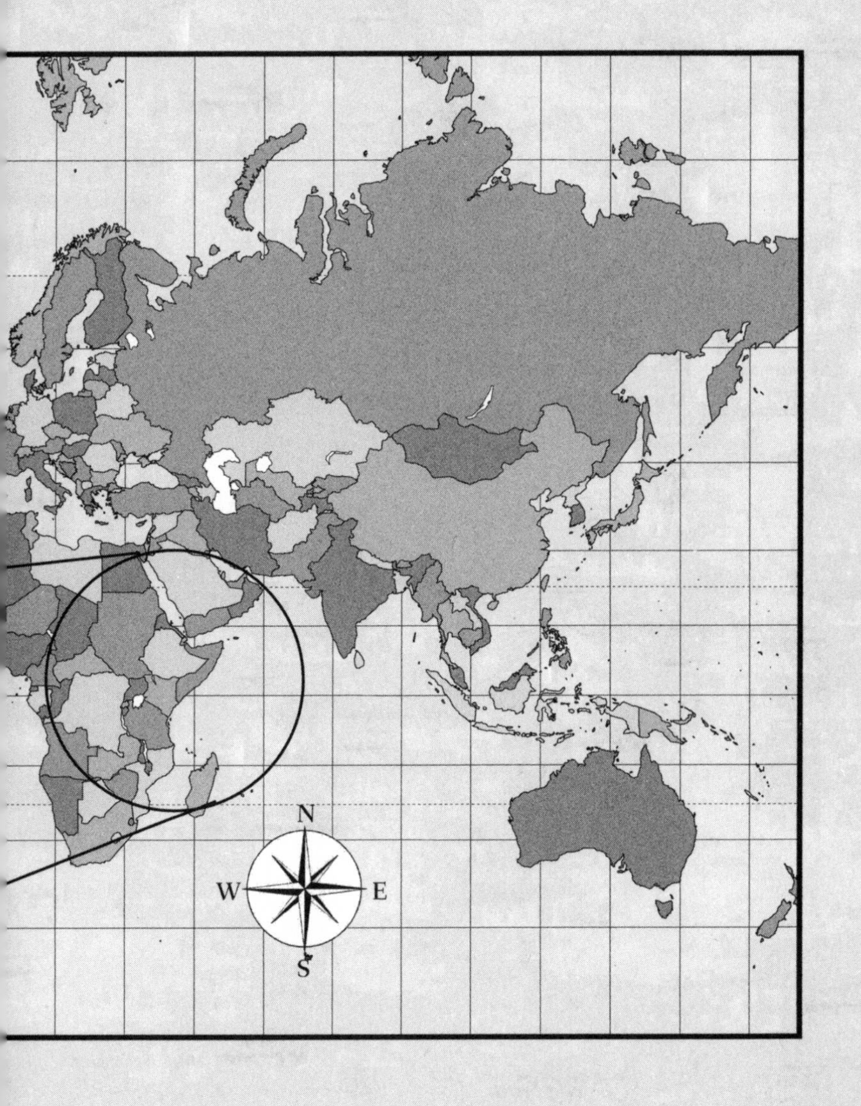
N
W
E
S

GLOBAL PROTECTION FORCE FILE ON

JACK STALWART

Jack Stalwart applied to be a secret agent for the Global Protection Force four months ago.

My name is Jack Stalwart. My older brother, Max, was a secret agent for you, until he disappeared on one of your missions. Now I want to be a secret agent, too. If you choose me, I will be an excellent secret agent and get rid of evil villains, just like my brother did.

Sincerely,

Jack Stalwart

GLOBAL PROTECTION FORCE INTERNAL MEMO:

HIGHLY CONFIDENTIAL

Jack Stalwart was sworn in as a Global Protection Force secret agent four months ago. Since that time, he has completed all of his missions successfully and has stopped no less than twelve evil villains. Because of this he has been assigned the code name "COURAGE."

Jack has yet to uncover the whereabouts of his brother, Max, who is still working for this organization at a secret location. Do not give Secret Agent Jack Stalwart this information. He is never to know about his brother.

Gerald Barter

Gerald Barter
Director, Global Protection Force

THINGS YOU'LL FIND IN EVERY BOOK

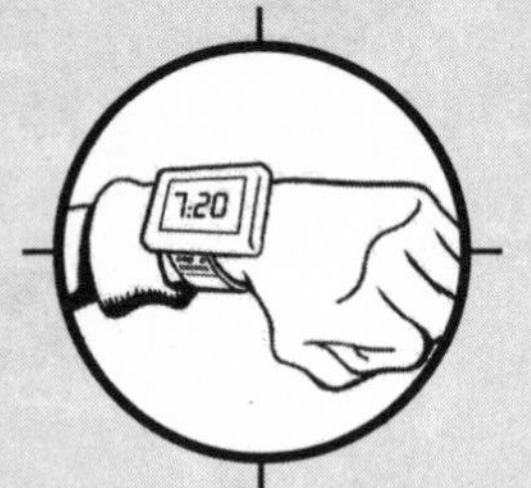

Watch Phone: The only gadget Jack wears all the time, even when he's not on official business. His Watch Phone is the central gadget that makes most others work. There are lots of important features, most importantly the C button, which reveals the code of the day – necessary to unlock Jack's Secret Agent Book Bag. There are buttons on both sides, one of which ejects his life-saving Melting Ink Pen. Beyond these functions, it also works as a phone and, of course, gives Jack the time of day.

Global Protection Force (GPF): The GPF is the organization Jack works for. It's a worldwide force of young secret agents whose aim is to protect the world's people, places, and possessions. No one knows exactly where its main offices are located (all correspondence and gadgets for repair are sent to a special PO Box, and training is held at various locations around the world), but Jack thinks it's somewhere cold, like the Arctic Circle.

Whizzy: Jack's magical miniature globe. Almost every night at precisely 7:30 PM, the GPF uses Whizzy to send Jack the identity of the country that he must travel to. Whizzy can't talk, but he can cough up messages. Jack's parents don't know Whizzy is anything more than a normal globe.

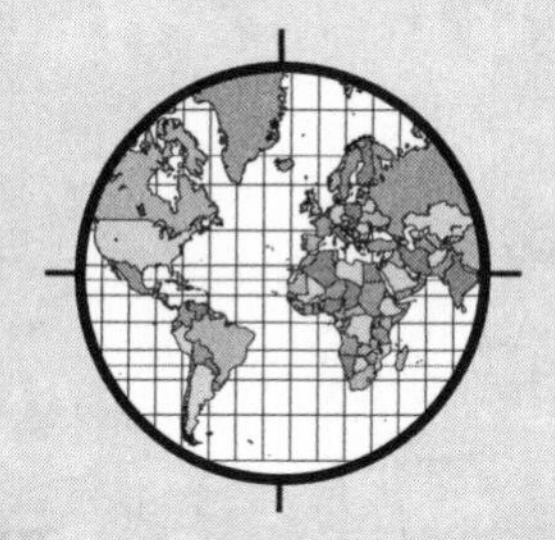

The Magic Map: The magical map hanging on Jack's bedroom wall. Unlike most maps, the GPF's map is made of a mysterious wood. Once Jack inserts the country piece from Whizzy, the map swallows Jack whole and sends him away on his missions. When he returns, he arrives precisely one minute after he left.

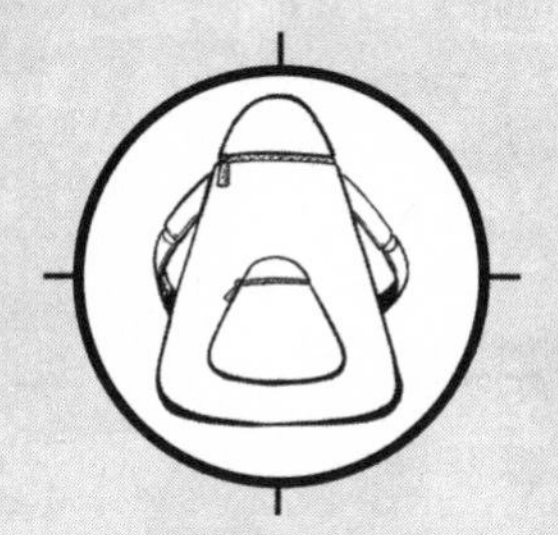

Secret Agent Book Bag: The Book Bag that Jack wears on every adventure. Licensed only to GPF secret agents, it contains top-secret gadgets necessary to foil bad guys and escape certain death. To activate the bag before each mission, Jack must punch in a secret code given to him by his Watch Phone. Once he's away, all he has to do is place his finger on the zipper, which identifies him as the owner of the bag, and it immediately opens.

THE STALWART FAMILY

Jack's dad, John

He moved the family to England when Jack was two, in order to take a job with an aerospace company. As far as Jack knows, his dad designs and manufactures airplane parts. Jack's dad thinks he is an ordinary boy and that his other son, Max, attends a school in Switzerland. Jack's dad is American and his mum is British, which makes Jack a bit of both.

Jack's mum, Corinne

One of the greatest mums as far as Jack is concerned. When she and her husband received a letter from a posh school in Switzerland inviting Max to attend, they were overjoyed. Since Max left six months ago, they have received numerous notes in Max's handwriting telling them he's OK. Little do they know it's all a lie and that it's the GPF sending those letters.

Jack's older brother, Max

Two years ago, at the age of nine, Max joined the GPF. Max used to tell Jack about his adventures and show him how to work his secret-agent gadgets. When the family received a letter inviting Max to attend a school in Europe, Jack figured it was to do with the GPF. Max told him he was right, but that he couldn't tell Jack anything about why he was going away.

Nine-year-old Jack Stalwart

Four months ago, Jack received an anonymous note saying: "Your brother is in danger. Only you can save him." As soon as he could, Jack applied to be a secret agent, too. Since that time, he's battled some of the world's most dangerous villains, and hopes some day in his travels to find and rescue his brother, Max.

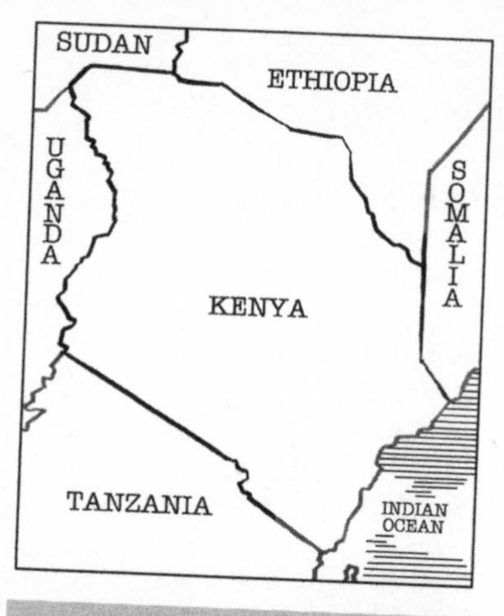

DESTINATION: *Kenya*

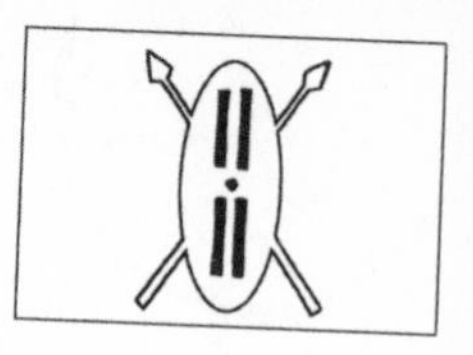

Kenya is on the continent of Africa, the second-largest continent in the world.

•

Nairobi is its capital city.

•

Kenya is a country with beaches, snow-capped mountains, and world-famous safari parks.

The sun rises at 7:00 AM and sets at 7:00 PM every day in Kenya, because it's located on the equator.

•

The Rift Valley, also called the "Cradle of Mankind," runs through Kenya. It's where many scientists believe 'early man' first evolved and lived.

•

Although Swahili is the national language, many people speak English.

ELEPHANTS: FACTS AND FIGURES

The word elephant means "great arch."

Elephants are the largest land mammals in the world. They can grow to be 13 feet tall and weigh 6 tons.

There are two kinds of elephants: African and Asian.

Elephants have twenty-six teeth, including their tusks. Tusks are made of ivory and have been sought after by hunters for thousands of years.

Elephants can live to be seventy years old. The main threat to their survival is poaching by man. During the 1970s and 1980s, more than eighty per cent of Kenya's elephant population was killed for its ivory.

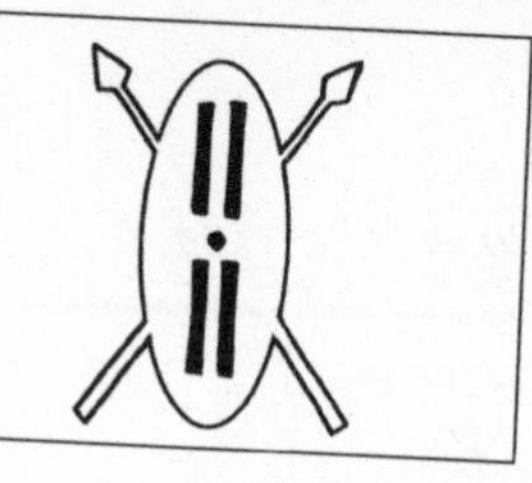

CULTURAL FILE: *The Maasai*

The Maasai are a tribe of semi-nomadic people living in eastern Africa.

◆

There are roughly 350,000 Maasai living in Kenya.

◆

They survive by herding and trading cows, goats, and sheep with other families.

The Maasai live on homesteads. Their homes are made of mud, sticks, grass, cow poo, and urine.

SECRET AGENT PHRASE BOOK FOR KENYA (SWAHILI)

SECRET AGENT GADGET INSTRUCTION MANUAL

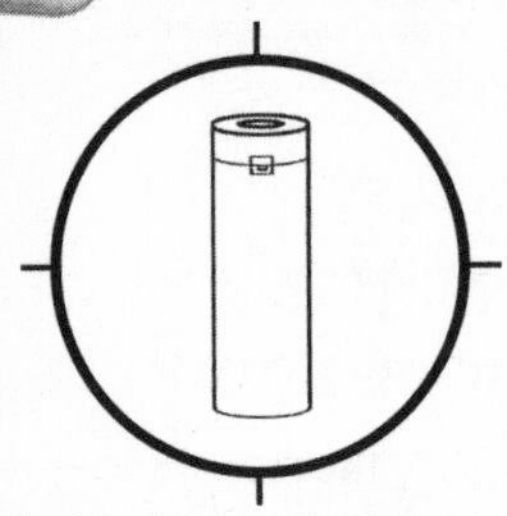

Hydro Pills: The GPF's Hydro Pills are an essential gadget for any secret agent working in extreme heat. Just shake two pills onto the tip of your tongue. Instantly, a burst of fresh water will fill your mouth. Swallow it and feel refreshed.

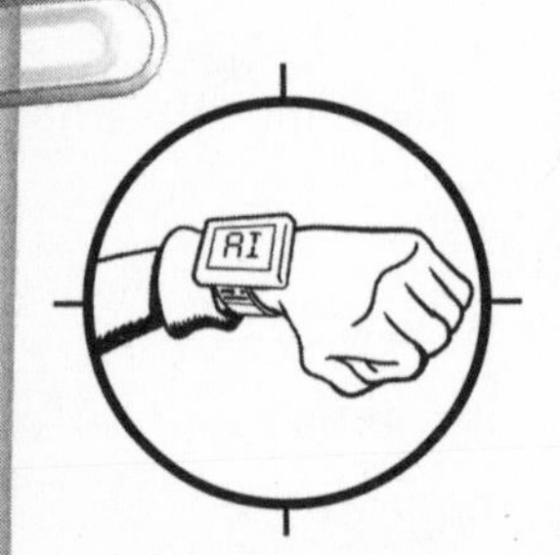

Anti-Intruder Alarm: Built into every secret agent's Watch Phone, the Anti-Intruder Alarm scans the surrounding area to detect when an intruder is nearby. Perfect when you need to get some rest and close your eyes for a while. You'll know there is someone around when your Watch Phone begins to vibrate. The Anti-Intruder Alarm can search up to fifteen feet away. To set the alarm, select the "AI" mode on your Watch Phone.

Transformation Dust:

When you need to change your appearance, even for a short while, use the GPF's Transformation Dust. Open the green packet and sprinkle some dust onto your head. At the same time, say what you want to become out loud. Within seconds, you will be transformed. To use on other people, just blow the dust over them for the same effect. Consult the back of this handbook for a complete list of transformation options.

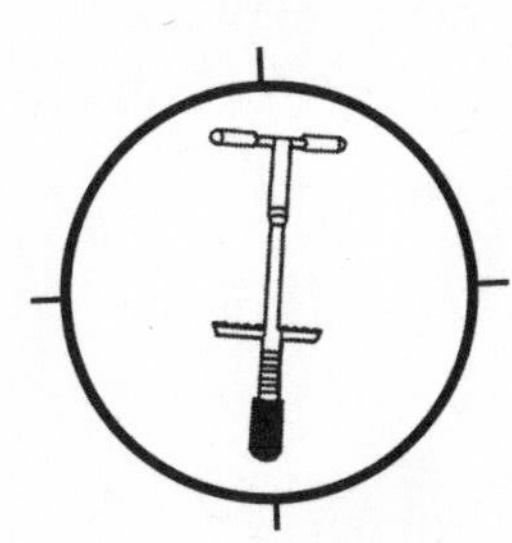

Power Pogo:

When you need to jump farther than your feet will take you, use the GPF's Power Pogo. The Power Pogo looks like an ordinary pogo stick, but it can catapult you up to fifteen feet into the air. Perfect when you need to get out of harm's way. Just step on and jump.

Chapter 1: The Letter

It was a warm summer evening and Jack and his mum were sitting at the kitchen table together. Jack's dad, John, was busy at work and wouldn't be home until later that night. As Jack took a bite of his cottage pie, his mum announced a bit of news.

"Did I tell you that we got a letter from Max?" she asked Jack.

"Really?" said Jack, only mildly interested. He figured it was another GPF letter designed to make his parents think Max was at a school in Switzerland instead of on assignment.

"It's over here," she said, jumping up from the table and going into the living room. As she rifled through the mail, she went on to explain: "And what's strange is that it's not from Switzerland. It's all the way from Egypt."

"Egypt?" said Jack, nearly choking on a piece of carrot. Why would the GPF fake a letter from Egypt? he wondered. They usually sent Max's letters from an address in Switzerland.

As he was thinking about it, Jack's mum began to read the letter aloud.

Dear Mum, Dad and JAck

You won't Believe iT, but I'M on a field trip iN Egypt. We're learNing about the History of This greAt coUntry and Seeing all Of the anciEnt monumEnts.

Please Tell JacK I miss Him.

Lots of love,

Max

"Isn't that sweet?" said Jack's mum. She was obviously proud of Max for making an effort to learn about the culture of a foreign country. "And look at how busy he is," she added, pointing to the letter. "He must have typed this really quickly."

Jack walked over to his mum and peered at the note where she was pointing. There was a curious mix of uppercase and lowercase letters.

"Can I borrow the letter, Mum?" he asked, trying to hide his excitement.

"Of course, sweetheart," she said. "But take care of it. I'm saving all of Max's letters for his special 'Switzerland scrapbook.'"

Before his mum could start talking again, Jack took the note and ran towards the stairs.

"Thanks!" he shouted as he climbed them two at a time. He reached his bedroom door and dashed inside to his bed. Climbing on top of his duvet, Jack stared carefully at the note.

It looked like a genuine letter. The way it was worded made it sound like Max. And the scribble at the end looked like Max's signature. But two things struck Jack as odd. Except for the handwritten scribble, it was created by a typewriter instead of a computer, and there was something going on with the size of some of the letters.

Jack reached under his bed and pulled out his Secret Agent Book Bag. Using his Watch Phone, he made contact with the GPF. Whenever a secret agent needed to use his or her gadgets when not on a mission, they could ask the GPF for special permission. Sure enough, the GPF quickly sent back the code SUPER CAR.

Jack laughed at how funny that was. He and his brother, Max, loved super cars like Ferraris and Lamborghinis.

Once Jack entered the code, the lock popped open. He reached inside and grabbed his Signature ID. The Signature ID was a three-dimensional rectangular box with a silver viewing screen inside. It was the only gadget in the world that could analyze someone's handwriting and identify its creator from a worldwide file. Whenever a secret agent needed to figure out whether an important document – like a ransom note or an ownership paper – was forged, they used the Signature ID.

For Max's other letters, Louise Persnall was the name given by the Signature ID. Jack knew that Louise was the GPF Director, Gerald Barter's, personal secretary. Hoping this time the letter was for real, Jack crossed his fingers and placed the glass square over the note.

Patiently, Jack waited for the Signature ID to do its work. When it was finished, he heard it beep. He took a breath and looked down at the screen. When he read what was there, his heart skipped a beat.

CREATOR: MAXWELL JOHN STALWART

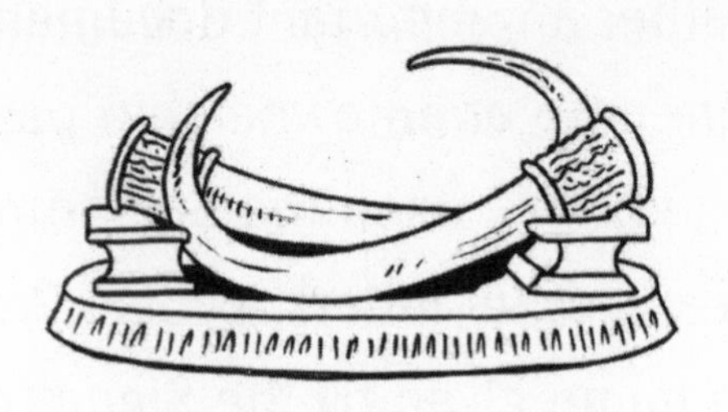

Chapter 2: The Code

Jack's insides were really tumbling now. He quickly put the Signature ID back in his Book Bag. Aside from an anonymous note telling Jack that Max was in trouble, he'd received no other communication about his brother in the past six months.

Jack took another look at the note and studied the uppercase letters that shouldn't have been there. He grabbed a pen and paper from his bedside table and wrote them down. There weren't many capital letters, so maybe they formed some sort of a code.

ABTMNNHTAUSOEETKH

Hmm, Jack thought as he stared at the jumble of letters. There was nothing obvious about anything to do with his brother.

When Jack was on a mission in Cambodia, he had received a clue about Max. His brother was supposedly working near a mummy in Egypt. After that tip, Jack did loads of research on mummies, but he still didn't have enough information to pinpoint his exact location.

Now, thought Jack as he stared at the code, he had been given a second chance. He was pretty sure that deep within the code was where Max was and why he was there. If Jack could solve it, he could probably help his brother. If he couldn't, well, Jack didn't even want to think about that.

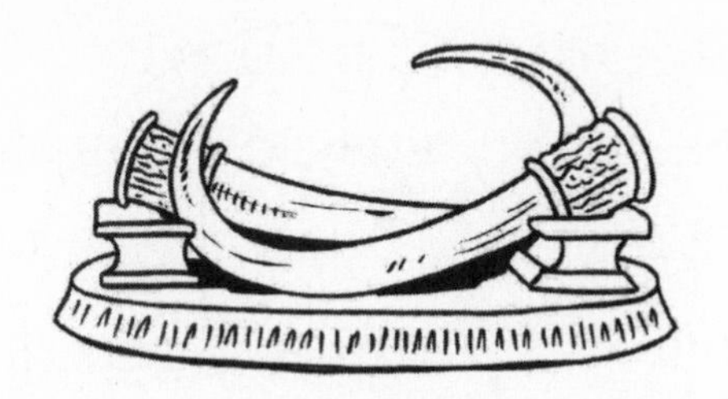

Chapter 3: The Assignment

Just then, Whizzy started to spin. Startled, Jack looked at the clock next to his little globe. It was already 7:30 PM.

Before Jack could think any more about Max, Whizzy coughed – Ahem! – and spat a jigsaw piece out of his mouth. Leaving his notes behind, Jack raced over to the spot where it landed. He looked at it carefully as he picked it up.

"Now where does this one fit?" he asked, carrying the piece to his Magic

Map. The wooden map of the world that hung on Jack's wall magically transported him away on his missions when he placed the correct country inside.

He lifted the piece up to the left of the map and tried to match it to Alaska. When that didn't work, he moved it to Canada. Going south through North

America and towards Mexico, he waited for the piece to slip in, but it didn't fit. He carried on, sliding the piece over South America, but still no match.

Getting excited that perhaps the country he was going to was actually Egypt, he picked up the piece and placed it over that country on the map. When it didn't match, he slid it over Central Africa and towards Africa's eastern edge. When he reached the coast, the piece fell in. The name "KENYA' appeared and then disappeared into the map.

"Kenya?" said Jack. He knew that Kenya was a place for safari holidays. Maybe a tourist is in trouble, he thought, as he grabbed his Book Bag. He dialed into his Watch Phone for the code of the day. As soon as he received the word – S-A-F-A-R-I – he punched it into the bag's lock and it popped open. Looking through the contents, he made a mental note of his Hydro Pills, Flyboard, and the Lava Laser.

Jack stuffed Max's note into his Book Bag and zipped it shut. He raced back to the

Magic Map, where the light inside Kenya was starting to grow. Knowing that he needed to be focused, Jack thought about Max one more time before sending thoughts of him out of his head.

When the yellow light coming from the African country had filled his room, Jack yelled, "Off to Kenya!" Then the light burst, swallowing him into the Magic Map.

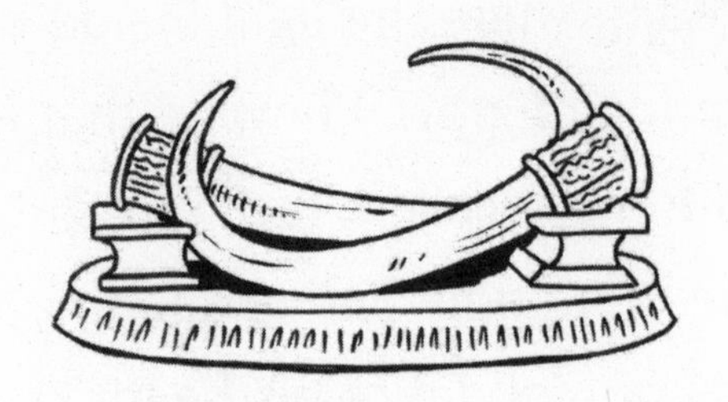

Chapter 4: The Savannah

When Jack arrived, he found himself alone in an open field. The tall grass under his feet was brown and dry. There was a khaki-colored dirt road to his far right, and the lone tree ahead was just that, all by itself.

From the looks of it, Jack figured he was in the savannah, one of the many types of landscape in Africa. Besides savannahs, Africa also had deserts and tropical rainforests, each with its own kind of exciting wildlife.

Jack opened his Book Bag and pulled out his Google Goggles. The GPF's Google Goggles looked like ordinary swim goggles but they enabled the wearer to see great distances both under the water and on land. He switched them to 'maximum' length, held them up to his eyes, and waited for them to focus.

Far in the distance he could see the animals of the plain. There was a herd of wildebeest making their way across a distant road. Beyond them was a family of giraffe. They were using their long tongues to eat leaves off of some prickly branches. An ostrich leaped into view and dashed across the savannah.

Scanning with the Google Goggles a further thirty degrees, Jack noticed a group of gazelle, a small deerlike animal. They were busy eating something off of the ground, while a group of patient lions watched their every move.

Jack looked at his Watch Phone. It had already adjusted itself to Kenyan time. Thankfully, it was after midday. Knowing that lions typically hunted in the cooler hours of the

morning and night, Jack wiped the sweat from his brow. The last thing he needed was an encounter with a pack of hungry wild animals.

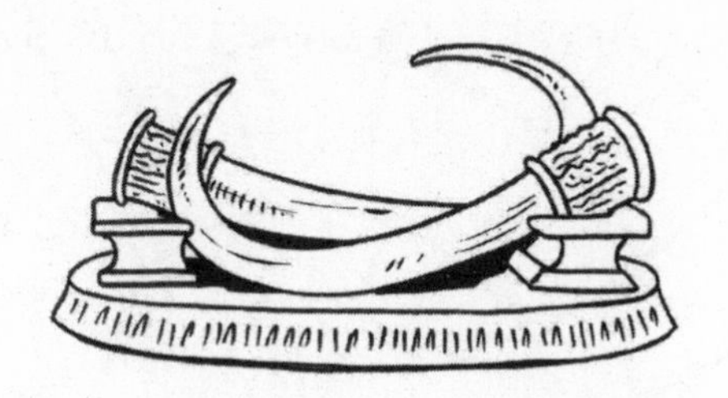

Chapter 5: The Bungling Brit

WHOOSH!

All of a sudden, there was a noise from above.

WHOOSH!

There it was again.

Jack dropped to his knees and aimed his Google Goggles at the sky. Sailing towards him was a red, yellow, and blue-striped hot-air balloon. Hanging underneath the balloon was an enormous wicker basket, and in the basket was a man wearing a floppy hat.

"Hello!" The man waved to Jack from his perch inside the balloon. Jack thought he sounded English.

"Hello!" he shouted again. His arms were flapping wildly as he tried to get control of the flying balloon. "I'm not very good with this thing!" he yelled as the balloon jolted up and down in the sky.

"I say," the man said. "Is your name Jack?"

Jack took a quick look around. Since there wasn't anyone for miles, he figured it was all right to say his name out loud.

"Yes!" he shouted back.

"Jolly good!" the man replied. "I'd hate to have flown all this way to find out your name was Frank!" At this silly joke, the man started roaring with laughter.

Jack watched the man try to steer the balloon to just above where he was standing. With a pull of a cord, he slowly lowered the craft. But instead of landing gently, the balloon's basket hit the ground and tipped over sideways.

"Ahhh!" the man screamed, tumbling out onto the dry grass.

"Are you OK?" asked Jack as he moved quickly to help the man. He was trying not to laugh, but the whole thing was *very* funny.

"Absolutely!" said the man, jumping to a standing position. He straightened his hat, quickly brushing the dirt from his trousers. "Just a bit more practice and I'll have this balloon-thing cracked!" he said.

"Where are my manners?" he exclaimed. "Trevor Dimbleby." He thrust out his hand. "Nice to meet you."

"Nice to meet you too, Trevor," said Jack, shaking the pilot's hand. "What seems to be the problem?" he asked, anxious to hear the reason for his mission.

"Chief Abasi is the one who sent for you," said Trevor. "He's the one with the problem."

"Chief Abasi?" asked Jack, curious to know who he was.

"Chief Abasi," Trevor explained, "is the chief of the local Maasai. He controls the bit of the Maasai Mara where my boss and I run a safari lodge."

Jack knew that the Maasai Mara was one of the biggest safari parks in Kenya and that the Maasai were a group of tribal people who lived off the land.

"Why don't we get a move on?" said Trevor, glancing at his watch. "It's two o'clock and I told the chief that I'd have you back in half an hour."

"Sure thing," said Jack. "But how are we getting there?"

Trevor paused and smiled. Jack looked at the balloon.

"You're joking," said Jack, not entirely confident with Trevor's piloting skills.

"Don't be a scaredy-cat," said Trevor as he started walking towards the craft. "I'm pretty much of an expert in that thing!"

Knowing that he had a few gadgets to help him out, Jack joined Trevor. Trevor was adjusting the temperature of the air, so the balloon could lift off the ground.

"Climb in!" he said to Jack.

Jack grabbed the edge of the basket and pulled himself over the side. He found a space next to the propane gas tanks and watched as Trevor yanked on a lever. A huge plume of flaming hot air shot up above Jack's head and they started to take off. Trevor tugged on the control again and the balloon began to rise even higher.

As they climbed into the sky, they caught a current of wind. The balloon flew upwards and to the east, taking Jack and Trevor to Chief Abasi and the mission ahead.

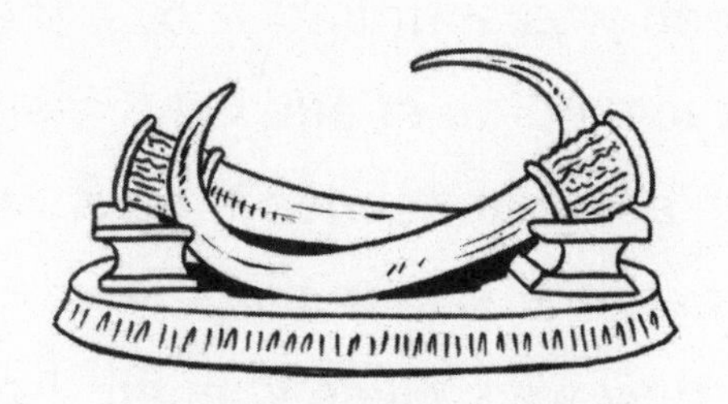

Chapter 6: The Homestead

After about twenty minutes, Trevor nudged him and pointed to something on the ground. "See that homestead over there?" he said. "That's where we're heading."

Jack lifted his Google Goggles once again, and surveyed the area around the village. There were five small homes made out of mud, a few small buildings, and three fenced-off pens for keeping cattle. Children were playing games, while the women were tending to chores. The entire homestead was surrounded by a thorny fence. It looked quiet and calm; not the kind of place that needed the services of an international secret agent.

When they were close enough, Trevor pulled a string to open the parachute valve. The parachute valve was on top of the balloon. It worked to let the hot air out, so the balloon would drop slowly to the ground. This time when the basket hit the earth, it did so gently. As it tipped over, Jack rolled himself out and Trevor followed him.

"So, where to now?" asked Jack, standing up.

"Over there," said Trevor, pointing to the gate. "Why don't you go ahead? I need to stay here and pack up the balloon."

As Jack walked through the gate and into the enclosure, he saw an African man coming out of one of the huts. He was wearing a red Maasai cloth around his shoulders, and some ornamental beads hung from his head and neck. With the use of a wooden walking stick, he slowly made his way over to Jack. Figuring this was Chief Abasi, Jack extended his hand to greet him.

"*Jambo*," said Jack. Jack knew that '*jambo*' meant hello in Swahili. "*Jina langu ni* Jack Stalwart."

The chief broke into an enormous smile. He was obviously pleased at Jack's attempt to speak the Kenyan language.

Although the Maasai had a language of their own, the man understood enough of what Jack said to respond.

"Welcome," he said, "to my homestead and to my country. I am honored that you have come." Jack was impressed by Chief Abasi's English. He was obviously a well-educated man.

Before Jack could ask, the man got to the point. "The reason I have called for you is that I have discovered a great problem on the Mara."

"What's wrong?" Jack asked. He was wondering what could be so bad in such a peaceful place.

"Why don't we take a walk?" he said, motioning for Jack to follow him out of the homestead. "Walking helps to clear my head," he added.

Jack paused, slightly confused. "OK," said Jack, guessing that whatever the chief had to show him was on the walk.

"Why don't you lead the way?"

The chief used his walking stick to swing round and made his way over to the gate. When Jack reached the gate, he glanced over at Trevor, who was busy chatting on his cell phone. It sounded

like he was speaking in Swahili. Spying Jack, Trevor stopped talking and waved. Jack waved back, too. Then he picked up his pace and followed Chief Abasi, who was already ten paces ahead.

Chapter 7: The Find

They were only minutes from the camp when Chief Abasi started to talk. "I am a great admirer of the GPF," he said. "I have been following the organization's work." The chief picked up his staff and stuck it into the ground.

Even though he lived in the middle of the African plain, Jack was amazed that Chief Abasi knew about the GPF. "How do you know about us?" asked Jack.

"I have my sources," he replied.

"Despite our simple way of living, I manage to stay on top of world events. Do you have any family?" he asked. Jack was surprised by the sudden change in conversation.

Jack paused for a moment, thinking about home. "I do," he said. "My mum, my dad, and my brother, Max."

"How old is Max?" said the chief.

"He's eleven," said Jack. In fact, his twelfth birthday was coming up. Jack thought about how happy he'd be if he could find Max and bring him home in time for his birthday celebration.

"So, where are we going?" asked Jack, deciding it was best to change the subject away from Max.

"I wanted to take you to the site of the problem, so you could see it with your own eyes," said the chief. He continued to walk ahead through the tall, dry grass. Just to the left, Jack could see eight elephants making their way across the savannah together.

Jack glanced at the temperature on his Watch Phone. It was 90°F. Feeling thirsty, he reached into the front pouch of his Book Bag and plucked out a clear plastic tube. Popping open the top, he shook out two pills and placed them onto the tip of his tongue. Within seconds, they dissolved into a concentrated burst of cool water. Instantly, Jack felt refreshed. These were the GPF's Hydro Pills – the only way a secret agent could stay hydrated in conditions like this.

"That's where we are headed," said Chief Abasi, lifting his staff and pointing it to a wooden building in the near distance.

Jack thought the building looked like a shed; the kind he had at home in his back garden. As they approached the building, Chief Abasi turned to Jack.

"I must warn you," he said. "What's inside may upset you."

"That's all right," said Jack, trying to sound brave.

The chief turned the handle on the shed door and pulled it wide open. He stood there waiting for Jack to take a look inside. As soon as Jack did, he immediately noticed two things. First, it didn't smell very nice. Secondly, there were lots of flies buzzing around. When his eyes finally adjusted, he knew instantly why Chief Abasi had called the GPF. Leaning against the walls were the ivory tusks of ten African elephants.

Sometimes tusks were taken from elephants that died of natural causes. But more often elephants were gunned down and killed so that the poachers could sell their tusks for money. Some people believed ivory had healing powers; others wanted to use it for ornamental carvings. Jack turned to look at the chief, who was still outside.

"Now do you understand?" asked Chief Abasi as he shook his head in sadness.

"I do," said Jack.

"The people who did this are not warriors," said the chief. "They are cowards."

"I agree," said Jack, who couldn't believe someone would do something like that. "I promise I'll find out who did this and make sure they never do it again."

"Thank you," said the chief. "Well then" – he stepped away from the shed – "why don't I give you some space? I'm sure that you have some work to do."

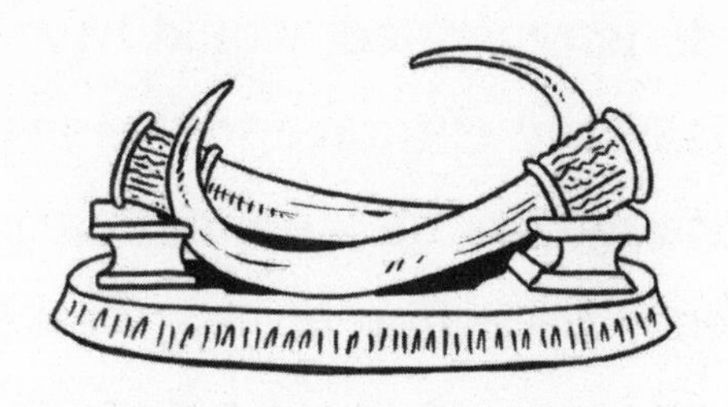

Chapter 8: The Clues

Once Jack had his bearings, he began to look around. The first thing he studied was the tusks themselves. There was nothing unusual about them, except stamped on each with black ink was the name of a faraway country. Jack figured these were the countries buying the tusks, but there was no clue as to who was selling them off.

When he was finished, Jack turned his attention to the outside. Whoever carried the tusks, he reasoned, would have left footprints at the entrance to the shed.

Sure enough, as he stepped outside, Jack spied a collection of footprints. One set of markings was too messy to make out; it was almost as if the person had been shuffling in the dust. The other, however, was so clear that Jack could see a squiggle on the sole of its shoe. A perfect opportunity for the GPF's Footprint Finder to do its stuff.

He grabbed the gadget from his Book Bag and turned it on by pulling on the ends of the yellow stick. Slowly, he moved the wand over the markings, giving it just enough time to register the print. Instantly, the Footprint Finder revealed the shoe's brand and size.

BOOT UNKNOWN, SIZE 11

Weird, Jack thought. The Footprint Finder almost never failed to identify a

shoe. It must be from a shoe that's custom-made.

He followed the footprints as they travelled from the shed to a nearby road. There they stopped at a set of four tire marks. Luckily for Jack, he didn't need a gadget to tell him what made these; he knew almost everything there was to know about cars. Based on the width of the axle and the tire's tread, these marks could only come from one kind of car: a four-wheel drive truck. Unfortunately for Jack, this was one of the most common types of vehicles on the African plain.

When Jack was finished, he joined Chief Abasi. "I'm done," he said.

"Did you find anything interesting?" asked the chief.

"Yeah," said Jack, "it looks like more than one person put the tusks in the shed. After that, they drove off in a four-wheel drive truck."

"Interesting," said the chief, considering what Jack had said. As if he was thinking about what that meant, Chief Abasi said,"I think you should meet Mr K next."

"Mr K?" asked Jack.

"His real name is Jasper Kendall," said the chief. "He runs Mr K's Safari Lodge, the largest safari camp in the Maasai Mara." "He and I have an arrangement of sorts," he added. "I let him run his business on Maasai land. In return, he lets us entertain and sell souvenirs to his guests."

"Do you think he'll know something about the poachers?" asked Jack.

"I am not sure," said the chief. "But what I do know is that Jasper is extremely well-connected; he has his finger into most things going on in and around the Mara."

"Great idea," said Jack, who agreed that a meeting would be wise. "Where exactly is Mr K's?"

"It's a short drive from the village," said the chief. "Trevor can take you and arrange for you to spend the night."

Jack hadn't even thought about the

time. He glanced at his Watch Phone. It was 5:30 PM. Since he knew the sun set at 7:00 PM, he didn't have enough daylight to solve the crime. He was going to have to spend the night at Mr. K's and carry on with his investigation in the morning.

As long as Jack stayed on a mission no longer than forty-eight hours, the GPF could return him to his bedroom at 7:31 PM. Beyond that they'd have to fake a reason for Jack being gone. That's what they did for Max. They engineered it so he was in a "boarding school."

"Shall we meet up again tomorrow?" suggested Jack.

"Yes," said Chief Abasi. "Trevor can pick you up in the morning and bring you back to the homestead."

"Great," said Jack. "That sounds like a plan."

Just then, Trevor pulled up in a jeep. Chief Abasi looked surprised at his arrival.

"Hello there," said Trevor, who was no longer wearing his hat. "I borrowed a car. I figured the two of you could use a lift."

"Stopped using the balloon, I see," said Jack, joking with Trevor. Jack climbed into the back of the car, leaving the front seat for the chief. "Aren't you coming?" he asked Chief Abasi, who was lingering behind.

"No thanks," he said. "I'd prefer to walk. Enjoy your visit with Mr K." He nodded his head to say goodbye and then turned to walk in the opposite direction.

Trevor crunched the gears, then slammed

his foot on the accelerator. As they tore off, Jack thought about Trevor – he hoped he was a better driver than he was a balloon pilot, but held on to his Book Bag, just in case.

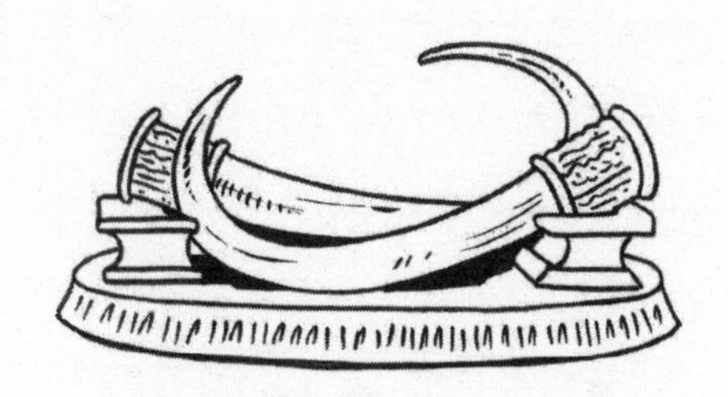

Chapter 9: The Safari Camp

Trevor and Jack had driven over the dusty plain for half an hour when Jack noticed a large campsite in the distance. There was an enormous wooden lodge in the middle surrounded by dozens of oversized green tents. Around the perimeter was an electric fence. Probably, Jack thought, to keep the lions away.

"That's Mr K's," said Trevor, pointing at the camp.

As they pulled up at the entrance, Jack

spied a large sign. It was written in big, bold letters. Inside the middle of the K was a drawing of a lion.

Beside the sign was an armed guard dressed in an olive shirt and trousers. Recognizing Trevor, he nodded and then let them pass. Trevor drove down the long path towards the lodge itself. He parked the jeep in a space marked 'reserved' and turned off the engine. Almost at the same time, a large man came out. Wearing a brown cowboy hat and a checked shirt, the man looked like he belonged more on the plains of Texas than that of Kenya.

"Hi there!" he bellowed. "How are you doing?" He sounded like he was from South Africa. Jack guessed that Trevor had called ahead and that he knew to expect them.

"So glad you could come," he said excitedly. "Welcome to my home. We call it Mr K's," he added, "after the first letter in my last name, Kendall." He looked over to Jack with a cheesy grin. "You get it?" he said.

Jack looked at the man and forced a smile. There was something about Jasper

that wasn't quite right. When he glanced down at his choice in footwear, Jack was shocked. He was wearing boots made with the skin of an endangered sea turtle.

"I thought killing sea turtles for their skins was against the law," said Jack, furrowing his brow in disapproval. He couldn't forget his duties with the GPF.

"These things?" he said, brushing Jack off. "These are so old," he said. "I've had them since before you were born!" Quickly changing the subject, Mr K carried on.

"Why don't you come in and have a look around?" Jasper slapped Jack on the back and led him down a gravel path towards the front door.

"Must be off," said Trevor as he climbed into the jeep. Trevor started the car up and began to back out. Before Jack could say goodbye, he'd sped away.

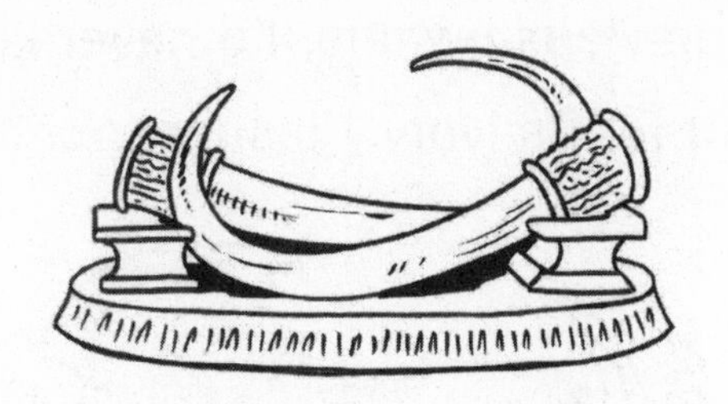

Chapter 10: The Meal

"Now," said Jasper, slapping Jack on the back a second time, "let's go inside!"

Jasper led Jack under the covered walkway and through the front door. When they entered the lobby, the first thing that caught Jack's eye was the elephant tusks. There were two decorated ivory teeth perched on a wooden stand in the corner.

Sensing that Jack was a bit stunned, Jasper explained. "They were given to me by the previous owners. I'd never kill an elephant for its ivory." Jasper coughed.

Uh-huh, thought Jack. He's wearing boots from an endangered species and he's got two tusks proudly displayed in the front hall of his lodge. Definitely, Jack decided, a guy who needs to be watched.

As they moved into the lodge, Jack noticed several young men doing a traditional Maasai jumping dance. Jack knew that Maasai showed their strength as warriors by jumping as high as they could. Remembering what Chief Abasi had said, Jack figured they were there to entertain Jasper's guests.

The two of them moved through the hall and towards a wooden deck outside. Almost as soon as he stepped onto the platform, Jack was overwhelmed by the wildlife. Black and white colobus monkeys were jumping from tree to tree. A spider the size of his dad's hand sat in the middle of its web just above Jack's head.

He walked over to the railing and looked over the edge. The deck was perched ten yards above a river below. There were some hippos sitting low in the water with their ears and eyes peeking out. A handful of baby crocodiles were scurrying across a log as their parents snapped up whatever food they could.

"Why don't you have a seat?" said Jasper, motioning for Jack to join him

at a round wooden table and chairs nearby.

Jack did just that, being careful to watch not only his surroundings but also his host.

"So," said Mr K, "Chief Abasi told me about those tusks. Shame about the elephants." At that comment, Jasper Kendall lifted his feet and placed them on the chair next to Jack. Since the shoes weren't that far away, Jack couldn't help but notice a squiggly line on the soles, just like the one he'd seen at the shed.

Jack's eyes widened. He needed to be careful. There was a chance he was sitting across from one, if not the leader of, the poachers. He cleared his throat.

"Yes," said Jack, trying to keep his cool. "It's terribly upsetting." He didn't want Jasper to know that he'd seen the boots. "Do you know who could have done this?" he asked.

"Gosh," said Jasper, almost sincerely. "I can't think of anyone."

"Well, why do you think someone would do it?" asked Jack.

"People round here don't make a lot of money," he explained, "and poaching is one of the best ways to get it."

Hmmm, thought Jack. Jasper wasn't admitting to anything. Jack didn't have enough evidence. He couldn't have him arrested just because of his boots. For all Jack knew, that squiggly line could be on any number of boots in the area. He was going to have to do better. He was going to have to catch Jasper Kendall in the act.

As Jack was thinking, a waiter came over and presented him with a plate of food. "Jambo," he said as he smiled down at Jack and placed the meal on the table.

"I ordered you some dinner," said Jasper, smiling.

Jack looked down at the skewer of alternating vegetables and gray meat.

"What is it?" asked Jack. He'd heard that in Africa people ate all sorts of things like zebra, crocodile, and wildebeest.

"An ostrich kebab," said Mr K.

Jack eyes popped open. The last thing

he wanted to do was eat that. Seeing Jack's reaction, Mr K roared with laughter.

"I'm actually not hungry right now," said Jack, trying to be polite. "Maybe I can take it back to my room?"

"Of course," said Jasper. He motioned to the waiter to wrap Jack's dinner.

"Just one more question," said Jack. "Have you noticed anyone acting strangely around here?"

"No one that I can think of," said Jasper.

"Well," Jack said, thinking he'd gotten all he was going to get out of Jasper, "I think I'd better head off to bed." He picked up his food.

"Let me show you to your room," said Jasper, standing to join Jack.

Jasper led Jack out of the dining room, through the lodge, and back outside.

Passing several large green tents in the compound, they arrived at one near the other end of the river bank.

"This is where you'll be sleeping tonight," said Jasper as he walked with Jack to a small wooden deck outside the tent opening. "I think you'll agree that our tents are pretty luxurious."

Jack pushed back the flaps to the tent. He walked in and couldn't believe his eyes. It was as big as his bedroom at home.

"There's a hot water bottle in your bed already," said Jasper. "It gets pretty cool at night. Electricity runs on a generator," he added. "Lights go off at eight-thirty and don't come on again until five in the morning."

Jack looked down at his Watch Phone. It was 7:30 PM. "Great," he said to Mr K, "that'll give me an hour to do some work."

“Sleep tight,” said Jasper as he let himself out. “Don’t let the bed bugs bite.” He gave Jack a big wink and pulled the flap to Jack’s tent closed behind him.

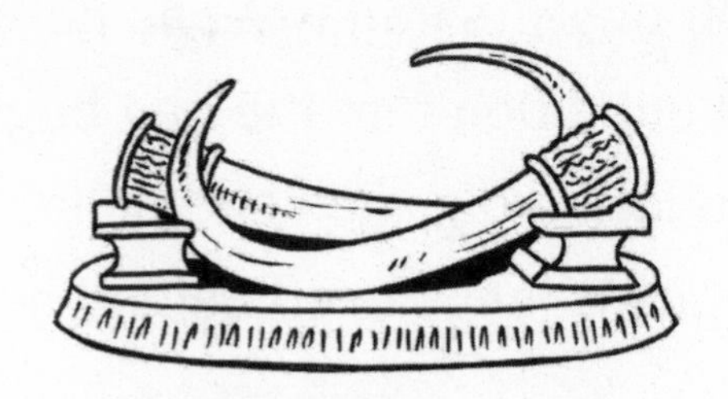

Chapter 11: The Breakthrough

Figuring he couldn't do any more on the case until tomorrow, Jack climbed onto the bed and got out Max's note. He looked at the uppercase letters again and thought about how to decipher the code. In his training, the GPF had taught him how to unscramble an "anagram." Anagrams were jumbled letters that when put back into the right order spelled a word.

He wrote out the letters again:

ABTMNNHTAUSOEETKH

Figuring the first thing Max would want to tell him was his location, he thought about places in Egypt where mummies could be found. There was the Valley of the Kings, but the letters in that word didn't match Max's code. He then thought about Thebes, where the Valley of the Kings was located. Sure enough, those letters were there. He crossed them out one by one.

A~~BT~~MNN~~H~~TAU~~S~~O~~EE~~TKH

Then he took the letters that were left and wrote them out again:

AMNNTAUOTKH

Now, Jack reckoned, there was a pretty good chance that what remained spelled the name of the mummy close to where Max was working. Jack tried to remember all the tombs found in the Valley of the Kings. There was the tomb of Seti and Siptah. Then there were at least seven tombs belonging to Ramses. But, those names didn't crack the code. And Jack couldn't remember any more. The only way Jack could solve this riddle was to look through his ancient Egypt book, which unfortunately was at home.

Knowing he couldn't do anything else, Jack put his brother's letter back in his Book Bag. Popping one of the GPF's Micro Brushes into his mouth, he swirled it around, letting it brush his teeth. When it was finished, it dissolved in his mouth. Since he didn't have any pajamas, Jack decided to sleep in his normal

clothes. He kept his Book Bag on for safekeeping.

After setting his Anti-Intruder Alarm, Jack crawled under the covers and lay on his side. Once he was comfortable, he closed his eyes and let his mind drift off to sleep. After all, he had some bad guys to catch in the morning.

Chapter 12: The Intruder

Sometime in the early morning, Jack was woken by a strong vibration on his wrist. Uh-oh, he thought. It was his Watch Phone's Anti-Intruder Alarm. It was telling him that there was somebody in the room.

Jack lay completely still and made sure his breathing was steady and slow.

Because it was dark and he couldn't see, the only senses he had were hearing and smell. He made use of both – as best he could – and tried to figure out who was sneaking around inside his tent.

Oddly enough, whoever it was, barely made a sound. Usually if someone was there, you could hear them breathe. Or smell their perfume. But there was no obvious scent. There was however a gentle noise. It sounded like it was coming from above Jack's head.

Sssssss.

Sssssss.

It was coming closer.

Sssssss.

Sssssss.

Thinking he had an idea of what it was, Jack slowly rose to a kneeling position, turning on his Everglo Light. Even though it looked like a small part of his Watch Phone, the Everglo Light could send a bright beam for at least fifteen feet.

At first he couldn't see anything because the intruder was the same green color as the tent, and Jack's eyes were getting used to the bright light. But when they did, he nearly jumped from the shock.

It was an African boomslang, one of the deadliest snakes in the world, and it was lowering itself down from a light in the ceiling, towards Jack on the bed below.

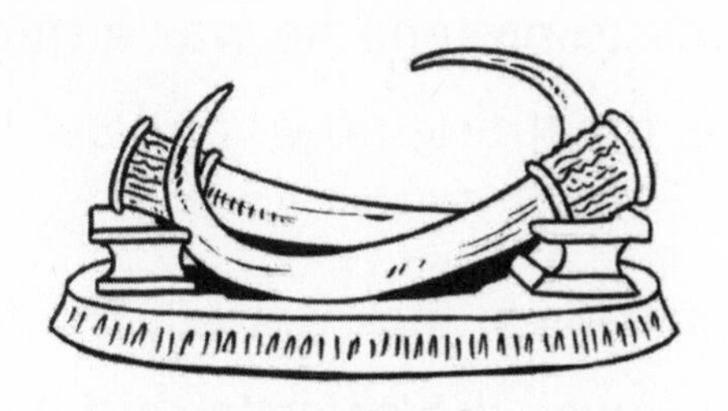

Chapter 13: The Idea

Before Jack could do anything, the snake had coiled itself to within three feet of his face. As Jack looked up, he stared into the snake's eyes. They were black and cold. Boomslangs were hemotoxic, which meant they could inject a poison that could make you bleed to death. And they were aggressive – one move from Jack and the snake would strike.

Since boomslangs were tree-dwelling snakes, the only way Jack could save himself was to pretend he was a tree. He slowed his breathing down and sat totally still.

Closing his eyes, Jack waited. The first thing he felt was the snake's cold body brushing against his nose. Then he felt it slide across his face. Slithering over his right shoulder, the snake made its way around his Book Bag and down the length of his back. Although it was travelling fairly quickly for a boomslang, it wasn't quick enough as far as Jack was concerned. It took all of his energy and concentration

not to move. But he had to remain still, or the snake would bite.

Finally, Jack felt the snake slide off of him and onto his mattress. As soon as he heard its heavy body thump onto the floor, he opened his eyes and looked around. The flap to his tent was wide open. The snake being in his room was no accident – somebody put it in there.

He looked over his shoulder and spied the snake's tail going under his bed. Thinking this was a perfect opportunity to escape, Jack carefully stood up and, using the beam from the Everglo Light, leaped as far as he could away from the bed. He hurried to the opening of the tent and stopped to look back. The boomslang was coming out from under the bed. Not wanting to come face-to-face with the creature again, Jack quickly headed out through the tent flap.

Now that he was outside, Jack decided the safest place for him was the lodge. Although the tents were dark, the main lodge was lit throughout the night. With the beam of his Everglo Light guiding him, he made his move. Just to his left, he could hear hippos burrowing themselves into the bank. From somewhere above came the strange sound of an unknown animal. Jack reckoned he'd seen enough of the local wildlife for one night, and hurried towards the main building as quickly as he could.

Chapter 14: The Transfer

"Jack!" said a voice from up ahead. Thanks to the glow of his torch, Jack could see that it was Jasper Kendall heading towards him. "What are you doing here?" he asked, seeming surprised. "It's a bit early to be out and about, isn't it?"

Yeah, right, thought Jack, who was thinking it was more than a coincidence that Jasper was up this early, too. Maybe he was the one who had put the snake in Jack's tent. Not wanting to let him in on his private thoughts, Jack just shrugged. "I wanted to use the lights in the main lodge to do some work."

"I see," said Jasper. He didn't seem convinced by Jack's excuse. "Why don't I take you there?" he said, leading Jack by the arm. "Shall I call Trevor and tell him that you'll be ready . . . a bit earlier than expected?"

"That would be nice," said Jack.

They soon reached the main building and Jasper phoned Trevor. It wasn't long before he arrived. He pulled up in the darkened car park. After all, it was only 6:00 AM.

"Morning," Trevor said. "I was thinking I'd take you on a safari drive. It's too early to see the old man anyway," he said, meaning Chief Abasi. "He's probably still asleep. But the animals, on the other hand, are just starting to wake up."

Jack thought that was a great idea. Any opportunity to learn about the animals, especially the elephants, could only help with the investigation. He also wanted to search for clues that would tie Jasper Kendall to the crime.

"Excellent idea," said Jack as he climbed into the front seat. Jack was impressed by Trevor's new Land Rover. He'd ridden in the same kind of vehicle once with his dad at a local motor show. "Nice car," Jack said.

"Thanks," said Trevor. "I got it in Mombasa."

Jack turned in his seat and looked at Mr K, who was waiting at the edge of the car park. He waved goodbye and gave Jack one of his cheesy grins. *I'll get you*, thought Jack as he waved back. *It's just a matter of time.*

Chapter 15: The Lion's Den

They'd driven for half an hour in darkness when Trevor piped up. "There's a place nearby where you can see the sunrise and watch the animals," he said.

"Sounds great," said Jack, who was looking forward to a break. After all, he'd had a stressful morning.

After a few minutes, Trevor shifted the car down a gear. "This is the place I told you about," he said as the Land Rover began to climb a steep hill. The car rocked back and forth as it made its way over some jagged rocks. "You'll love the view from up here." He sounded very excited.

When the car heaved over the ridge, Trevor drove onto a flatter piece of land. With the sun beginning to rise, Jack could make out some trees lining the top of the hill. Dotting the ground were what looked like small- to medium-sized rocks. Trevor put the car into neutral.

As Jack looked around, he noticed something odd. There weren't any animals here. What was Trevor thinking? Jack said to himself. Then he heard what sounded like a lion's yawn.

Squinting, Jack could just make out some larger shapes underneath the trees. As the sun's light grew brighter by the second, things became clearer. There were six adult lions lying down on their bellies. Four of them were female; two of them were male. Jack knew this because two had magnificent manes of hair. Jack wouldn't have been so worried if it weren't for the fact that the Land Rover didn't have any doors on its sides.

"Trevor," said Jack, not wanting to sound scared, "isn't this a bit risky? I'd like to see some wild animals," he added, "but maybe not lions that are this close."

Trevor turned to Jack. "Get out," he said. But he didn't say it kindly; he said it with a sinister snarl.

"What?" said Jack, who wasn't sure he'd heard Trevor correctly.

Trevor opened the glove box in front of Jack. He reached in and pulled out a knife in a brown leather sheath. As Trevor slid the cover off with his other hand, he glared at Jack.

"You heard me," he growled. "Get out! And if you don't," he added, "I'll have to use this." Trevor waved the knife in Jack's face so he could see its razor-sharp edge.

Jack was stunned. What was going on? Where was the friendly Trevor he knew? And why was he holding a knife in Jack's face?

"I've been collecting these tusks for weeks," Trevor explained. "And then Chief Abasi had to go and find them on one of his little "walks." Now, I have to find more ivory," he explained. "My Far Eastern buyers are desperate for their goods, and I don't need the likes of you getting in the way."

Jack almost couldn't talk from surprise. "But I thought—" said Jack, thinking about Jasper Kendall and the bootprints he'd found at the shed.

"What, that Jasper Kendall had something to do with it?" he snarled. "That guy couldn't pick his nose if it weren't for me! I knew a little busybody like you would come sniffing around the shed if it was ever found," he explained, "so I put Jasper's boots on and made some nice tracks. Looks like it worked. Otherwise you wouldn't be here with me."

Jack thought back to when he first met Trevor. Trevor made it seem like he was a bit of a clown . . . the floppy hat, his wacky way of piloting the balloon, the way he talked. That was all just a trick to make Jack think he was a nice guy, not a cold-hearted ivory poacher!

"I tried to get rid of you last night," Trevor went on, "but somehow you managed to escape. This time," he added, with a snigger, "I think the lions will do a better job."

Of course, Jack thought. Trevor must have snuck back into the camp and put the snake in his tent. It would have been very easy for him to do. After all, they were used to seeing him around Mr K's.

Jack didn't have much time. He pulled his thoughts together. "But how can you kill innocent animals?" he said, trying to distract Trevor. As he spoke, he took what looked like a coin out of his pocket and let it drop to the floor of the Land Rover.

"There's only one simple answer to that question," said Trevor. "Money . . . Now get out!"

Jack thought about his options. Unfortunately for him there wasn't a

gadget that could get him out of a situation involving a knife. There was only one thing to do, and that was to climb out of the car and take his chances with the lions.

Chapter 16: The Trees

With the sun nearly awake, Jack could see finally what he was up against. The lions were now standing on all fours. They were watching Jack as he got out of the car.

"Trevor," said Jack as he stepped out and onto the dirt. "I'm warning you. Don't do this. African elephants are already endangered. Killing more will just make matters worse."

Trevor laughed one last dramatic laugh – he didn't care at all. He revved the engine and slipped it back into gear, then peeled away from the spot and left Jack without any protection.

"ROOOOAAARR!"

Quickly, Jack turned around to see one of the male lions licking his chops. The females were gathering together. Jack knew that lions hunted in the morning hours, which meant that they were probably looking at Jack as easy food. He didn't have much time to act. He was going to have to get out of there before they attacked.

Taking off his Book Bag, Jack crouched on the ground. The female lions were beginning to surround him, since they did all of the hunting. With animals on all sides, there was only one gadget that could help Jack.

The GPF's Power Pogo was a pogo stick like no other. With one bounce, it could catapult you up to fifteen feet high.

Jack grabbed the life-saving gadget, strapped his Book Bag back on, and placed his hands and one foot on the Power Pogo. He looked at the lions. The female lions were inching closer while the male lions were waiting patiently under the trees.

"ROOOOAAARR!

Like lightning, the lionesses sprang into action, pushing with their strong hind legs to leap forward. They were charging at top speed in an attempt to bring Jack down! Quickly, Jack lifted his other foot and jumped onto the pogo stick for its first bounce. When it hit the ground, it flew up into the air.

BOING!

One of the lion's paws just missed Jack's feet as he rocketed into the sky,

then came crashing back to the ground. Luckily for Jack, he landed just to the right of the pride of lions, who were scrambling to reach him.

BOING!

This time he sprung even further. One more time, thought Jack, and he'd be next to the trees.

BOING!

The Power Pogo thrust him towards an acacia tree. As he came down, he grabbed onto one of its branches and held on. His feet were dangling down. The Power Pogo fell to the dusty ground, almost hitting one of the male lion's head.

"ROOOOAAARR!"

The male lion wasn't happy. Using the strength in his arms, Jack pulled himself onto a branch inside the tree. Perched there for safety, he glanced down at the lions below. Their "easy" breakfast had

completely disappeared. Jack smiled. Things were finally going his way.

Taking a moment, Jack remembered what Trevor had said. He needed more ivory. Guessing that's where Trevor was off to now, Jack looked at his Watch Phone and punched a few buttons. The Transponder that he'd dropped in Trevor's car was showing a location just ten miles away. Since the blinking light wasn't moving, Jack started to worry.

Jack had to get to Trevor before he killed another elephant. He looked out the other side of the tree from where he was sitting. There was a gentle drop from the hill to the savannah. Peering through the branches at the lions, he saw that they had given up on catching him. The pride was heading somewhere else in search of food. Lowering himself down, he collected his gadget, packed it away, and scrambled through some bushes to the top of the slope. He slid down it towards the flatter land below. Perfect terrain, Jack thought, for one of his favorite gadgets. It was the GPF's Flyboard and it was waiting for him in his Book Bag.

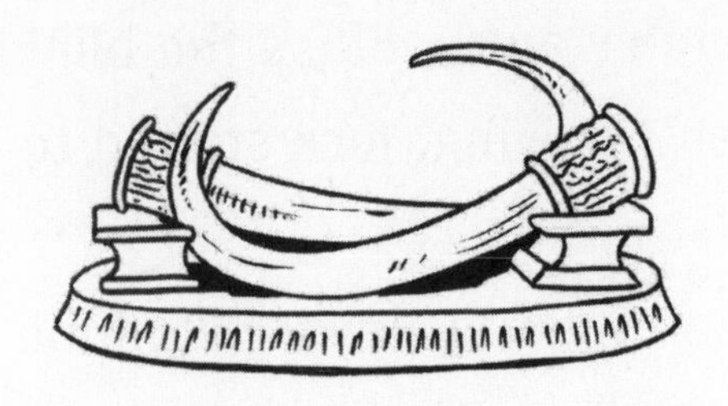

Chapter 17: The Confrontation

After snapping the Flyboard together, Jack hopped on. Punching the "air" button on his Watch Phone, the jets fired up and Jack and the Flyboard took off. Given the distance and the speed he was travelling, Jack worked out he would arrive at the Land Rover within moments.

He soon saw Trevor's car up ahead, and it looked as if he was just in time. Directly across from the car was a family of elephants. They were bumping into

trees and grasping at branches with their trunks. Trevor was standing up in the vehicle with another man. It looked like the waiter from Mr K's lodge – the one who served Jack his ostrich kebab. So, that's Trevor's accomplice, thought Jack. That's who left the set of messy footprints at the shed.

The two men were wearing hunter's vests and pointing their guns towards one of the female elephants.

"No!" screamed Jack, urging the Flyboard to go faster.

But Trevor and the other man couldn't hear him; he was still half a mile away. They leaned their ears on the guns and looked through the sights.

"Stop!" yelled Jack.

At that last shout, Trevor must have heard him, because he lifted his head and looked in Jack's direction. By the time both men had registered Jack's arrival, he was nearly there.

"You?" snarled Trevor, clearly unhappy to see that Jack had escaped a second time. "What are you doing here?" he yelled. "Go away! We have some business to do."

"No, you don't," said Jack. "I'm not going to let you kill these elephants!"

"Oh, yeah?" said Trevor, swinging his gun so that it was now pointing at Jack.

Jack flinched.

"Hapana!" the other man yelled in Swahili, aiming his gun at Jack, too. The female elephant sensed the danger and was leading her family in the other direction.

As Trevor put his head down on the gun, ready to fire, Jack pulled his Lava Laser out of his bag. Even though it looked like an ordinary pencil, the GPF's Lava Laser was powerful enough to make metal burn as hot as lava, so that whoever was touching it would have to drop it.

Trevor put his finger on the trigger. Jack fired the Lava Laser. A ray of light shot out of the gadget and struck the metal on Trevor's gun. Almost instantly, the gun started to glow orange with heat, burning Trevor's hands.

"Owwww!" he yelled in agony, dropping the hot metal object.

"Hapana!" the Kenyan man yelled, lowering his face to his gun. He was about to fire.

But Jack and the Lava Laser got him, too.

"Ahhhh!" he howled, shaking his hands and trying to cool them. Jack guessed that a cry of pain sounded the same in Swahili as it did in English.

Realizing that they weren't going to kill either Jack or the elephants, the two men dropped in their seats. They were going to start up their car. Trevor tried to turn the key in the ignition, but his hands were too sore and blistered to touch anything.

"Arrgh!" he yelled, obviously disgusted with what was happening.

Panicked and desperate, the two men jumped out. They started to run in different directions. Jack reached into his pocket and pulled out his Transformation Dust. He opened the packet and directed the Flyboard over to the waiter from Mr K's lodge.

"Rhinoceros," Jack said as he blew some of the dust onto the man's face.

"Kifaru?" the waiter said, repeating the word for rhinoceros in Swahili. As the dust flew into his face, he coughed, spat, and shook his head. Almost instantly, he was transformed into one of the most hunted and endangered African animals – the black rhino. Jack then sped over to Trevor, who was sprinting as far as he could, but not fast enough.

"Please, don't!" Trevor screamed as he looked at his accomplice and realized what Jack was about to do. "Noooo!"

"Elephant," said Jack as he blew the dust. On that very spot, Trevor was turned

into a two-ton female elephant. Trevor lifted his trunk and blew a sound of fury.

"Now," said Jack, pleased with himself. "Let's see how you like being a hunted animal."

Although Jack would have loved to keep them that way forever, he knew the GPF's

Transformation Dust would only last an hour. No problem, thought Jack. It was a clever enough way to catch the poachers and teach them a lesson at the same time.

Jack phoned the Kenyan police, who arrived fairly quickly, but not soon enough for both Trevor and the waiter, who were being sniffed at by a pack of hyenas.

Once the criminals had changed back to themselves, the police officers arrested them and hauled them off.

"You're going to pay for this, kid!" yelled Trevor as the van door shut behind him.

No, thought Jack to himself. *You're the one who's going to pay.*

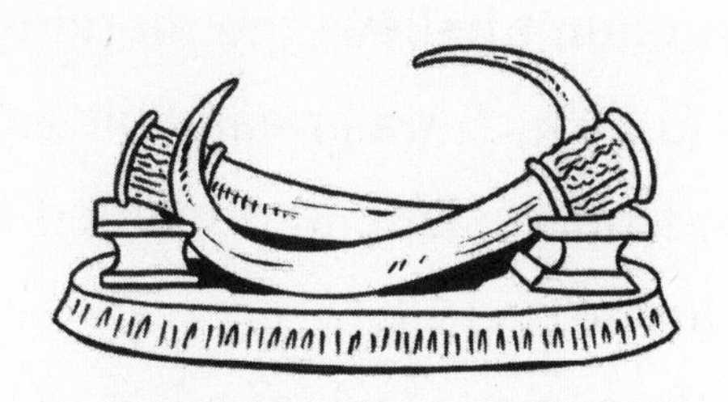

Chapter 18:
The Find

Now that the bad guys were locked up, it was time to pay a visit to Chief Abasi. After all, Jack was supposed to meet him this morning and he was already late.

He jumped on his Flyboard and headed for the homestead. As he zoomed towards the gate of the Maasai village, Chief Abasi came out of a hut to greet him.

"Hello, Jack," he said, using his stick to walk over. "Has anything happened since we last spoke?"

"You wouldn't believe the morning I've had!" said Jack. "I was nearly bitten by a poisonous boomslang and mauled by a pack of lions!"

Chief Abasi's eyes widened at the news.

"But everything is all right now," said Jack. "I caught Trevor and a waiter from Mr K's trying to kill more elephants. They were the poachers responsible for those tusks in the shed."

Chief Abasi wobbled on his feet before taking a step back. He was obviously in a bit of shock. "I can't believe this," said the chief. "Trevor was a trusted friend of the Maasai people."

"Unfortunately, I don't think Trevor was anybody's friend," said Jack. "He pretended to be nice so nobody would suspect him of the crime. But Trevor's locked up now, so he'll have plenty of time to think about what he's done."

Chief Abasi shook his head. "Well then," he said to Jack, "we owe you and the GPF a great deal of thanks. You've rid our area of some nasty poachers and the elephants here in Kenya will be safer thanks to your efforts."

"No problem," said Jack, who was pleased with himself. "I'm just happy I could help." He held out his hand. "If there are any more problems, give me a call."

“I will,” said the chief, putting his hand in Jack’s. “Be safe in your travels. And to help guide you, I would like to give you a gift.” Chief Abasi left Jack for a moment and walked to his hut.

When he returned, he had a beaded necklace in his hands. “This is for good luck,” he said, handing it to Jack. “And for the luck of your family.”

Little did the chief know, thought Jack, how much luck the Stalwart family actually needed. As Jack looked down at the red necklace, he thought about his brother Max.

Jack took the object and smiled. "Thank you," he said as he placed it around his neck. "I'll treasure it always." Jack waved goodbye to the chief and stepped on his Flyboard.

Leaving the homestead behind, he flew across the hot plains and stopped near a cluster of bushes. He packed his gadget away, and after pushing a few buttons on his Watch Phone, closed his eyes and yelled, "Off to England!" Within moments Jack was transported home to his bedroom.

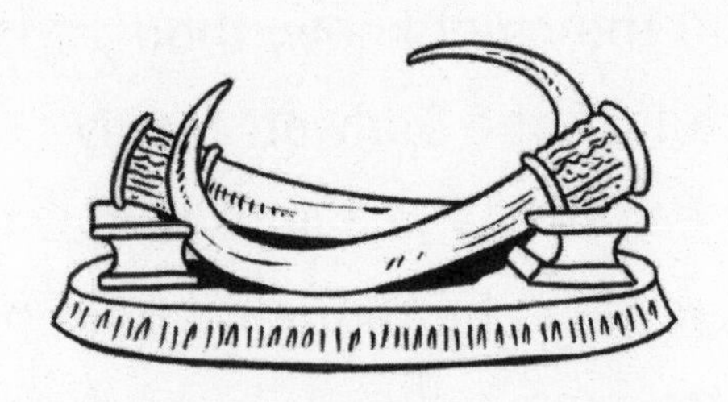

Chapter 19: The Breakthrough

As soon as he arrived, Jack grabbed the book on ancient Egypt off of his bookcase and sat down with it and his brother's note. He flicked through the pages and found one with a list of all the tombs in Thebes, then laid out what was left of the code again:

AMNNTAUOTKH

Then Jack compared the tomb names with the letters in the code. The first name on the list was Merenptah, but that didn't work. Scrolling down, he tried to match every name with the anagram, but nothing seemed to fit. By the time he got to the last name, he didn't hold out much hope. Jack wrote out the letters anyway. After all, King Tut was the most famous mummy in the world.

TUTANKHAMON

As he was writing, he realized that nearly every letter fit with the anagram from Max's note. The only problem was that in the book Tutankhamun was spelled with a "u' instead of the "o' that was in Max's code. Drat, thought Jack. Maybe he was wrong. Maybe the letters spelled another mummy's name.

But it was so close. Perhaps, wondered Jack, there was another spelling. He knew this was common when it came to ancient names for people and places. Feeling excited, he raced to his computer and punched the name Tutankhamun into the search field. Three different spellings for the famous boy king showed up.

One of them was spelled with an "o."

Jack looked down at the necklace that Chief Abasi had given him. "Thanks," he whispered to the man who had given him the necklace and his incredible good luck.

TUTANKHAMON

It was a perfect match.

The Puzzle of the Missing Panda: CHINA

BOOK 7

Read the first chapter here

Chapter 1:
The Throw

Jack and his mum drove into the village hall car park. “I’ll pick you up in an hour,” she said. Jack opened the door, quickly waved “goodbye” and shut the door behind him. His mum had some grocery shopping to do. She put the car in gear and pulled away.

Every weekend, twenty kids including Jack met to learn judo from Mr Baskin, one of the best judo instructors in Great Britain. Judo is a type of martial art from Japan. Thanks to Mr Baskin, Jack had already earned his yellow belt. Not only was judo recommended by the GPF, it was something that Jack loved doing.

As he entered the building, he spotted his friends Richard and Charlie. They were also dressed in the judo uniform called a *judogi*. A *judogi* was a white jacket and trousers with a special belt tied around the waist. Jack walked over to say “hi,” but almost at the same time Mr Baskin yelled out to the class.

"OK, everyone!" he said. "Let's begin."

Jack went over to the edge of the mat, tidied up his *judogi* and tossed off his flip-flops. Then he, Richard, Charlie, and the rest of the class stepped onto the mat and waited for instructions.

"Floor work!" Mr Baskin said. "Commando style!" he added.

Everyone knew what to do. Hurrying to one side of the mat, the first row of students dropped to the floor and lay on their stomachs. Then they used their elbows to pull themselves across the mat, like soldiers in a trench. Almost as soon

as they'd finished, Mr Baskin shouted another command.

"Cartwheels!" he said.

Jack could hear the rest of the boys sigh in dread. While the girls in the class loved doing cartwheels, it was difficult for Jack and the other boys to get their legs around.

Jack did his best, and when he'd made it across the mat, he heard Mr Baskin call everyone back to the center. They returned to the middle, sat back on their heels and listened carefully to what the teacher had to say.

"Can anyone tell me what *hansoku-make* means?" he asked.

Jack knew the answer. He raised his hand. "Disqualification," he offered when Mr Baskin called on him.

"Yes!" said Mr Baskin, pleased that the first answer of the day was a correct one.

"And what causes a disqualification?" he asked.

Charlie's hand shot up. "Putting your fingers up an opponent's sleeve," he answered.

"Well," said Mr Baskin, "that wouldn't cause a *hansoku-make*. Can anyone tell me what putting your hands up an opponent's sleeve *would* cause?"

Richard raised his hand. "A *shido*?"

"Excellent!" Mr Baskin said. "Yes, putting your fingers up someone's sleeve would cause a *shido*, or small penalty. "What else?" he asked, searching for other means of disqualification.

A girl a few kids back from Jack raised her hand. Although Jack didn't know her name, he knew that she was more skilled than him because she was wearing an orange belt.

"Punching someone in the face," she replied, with a naughty smile.

The instructor smiled back. "Good one, Charlotte," he said. "Any other ideas?"

Charlie raised his hand again. "What about if you wear metal or jewelery?" he asked.

"Yes!" said Mr Baskin, excited that his class had been paying attention to previous lessons.

Another girl raised her hand too. Jack recognized her as Emma, a girl who lived a few streets over from him. She was eight years old.

"Biting someone?" she offered.

"Excellent," said Mr Baskin. "All of those things – punching, wearing metal, and biting – can lead to disqualification.

"Now," he continued, moving on from the questions and answers, "today, we're

going to learn a new throw. It's called a *harai goshi*. It's known as the 'sweeping hip throw' and is an excellent move that can have a number of results."

He got up and, with the help of Tim, a thirteen-year-old boy who sometimes assisted him, showed the class how it was done. When the demonstration was over, the instructor told everyone to find a partner. Richard and Charlie nabbed each other first, which left Jack alone, but not for long. Charlotte, the girl with the orange belt, turned up in front of him almost instantly.

"Wanna be my partner?" she asked.

Jack looked around for another partner, but everyone had already paired up. He never liked practicing with girls. He didn't like the thought of hurting them.

"OK," he said reluctantly. "Shall we get started?"

Jack and Charlotte bowed to each other. As Jack reached for Charlotte's sleeve, she moved quickly. She grabbed his right arm, twisted in towards his body, lifted him up on her back, then grabbed his trouser leg and threw him on the floor.

THWACK!

Jack's body hit the mat hard. He'd never been thrown by a girl before. He looked up at Charlotte, who was standing above him, arms crossed, with one of those know-it-all grins on her face. Hopefully his friends hadn't seen what had happened.

Pretending that it didn't bother him, Jack got up and coolly said, "I let you do that."

He and Charlotte faced each other for another match. As they tidied their *judogis*, Jack was going through the moves in his head. Just as they were about to begin, Mr Baskin shouted for everyone to find a new partner. Without saying a word, Charlotte flicked her ponytail and strutted off with her nose in the air.

Before Jack could think about getting back at Charlotte, Adam stepped in front of him. He and Adam were in the same class at school. The two of them bowed to each other, and after a pretty good wrestle, Jack threw Adam to the floor. Then they repeated the move and Jack let Adam do the same to him.

They practiced over and over, so that by the end of that session, Jack was pretty good at performing the *harai goshi*. Now all

he had to do was find Charlotte again. He'd throw *her* this time round. But unfortunately that wasn't going to happen – at least, not today.

"Gather up!" yelled Mr Baskin, motioning for everyone to sit in front of him in a row.

Jack and the rest of the students sat on their heels across from Mr Baskin, who

congratulated them on their hard work. As soon as they were dismissed, Jack, Richard, and Charlie gathered up their things and walked outside.

While they were waiting for their mums, they talked about lots of things, like whether they were going to enter the next judo competition. (Richard was, Charlie wasn't, and Jack thought he might.)

When Jack's mum pulled up, Jack said goodbye to his friends and climbed into the car, which was filled with groceries.

When he got home, he helped his mum put away the food and then played a car-racing game on his Xbox. Sometime after dinner, he kissed his mum good-night – his dad was working all weekend again – and made his way upstairs to his room.

As he got to his door, Jack flipped the

sign outside to "KEEP OUT." Although he loved his mum, he didn't want her just barging in. After all, top-secret stuff happened in there. And it was nearly 7:30 PM.